Robinson Crusoe

Based on the Novel by Daniel Defoe
Adapted by Michael Sandler

SCHOLASTIC INC.

New York   Toronto   London   Auckland   Sydney
Mexico City   New Delhi   Hong Kong   Buenos Aires

Illustrations
Natalie Ascencios

Text copyright © 2003 by Scholastic Inc.
Illustrations copyright © 2003 by Natalie Ascencios.
All rights reserved. Published by Scholastic Inc.
Printed in the U.S.A.

ISBN 0-439-59780-3

SCHOLASTIC, SCHOLASTIC ACTION, and associated logos and designs are trademarks and/or registered trademarks of Scholastic Inc.

LEXILE is a registered trademark of MetaMetrics, Inc.

12 13 14 15   23   12 11 10

Contents

Welcome to This Book

Have you ever thought your life was boring?
Have you ever wished to have an adventure?
Well, be careful what you wish for!

Robinson Crusoe went looking for adventure and got more than he wanted. His parents had warned him about going to sea. They told him that it was dangerous. But he didn't listen.

Now, he is stuck alone in the middle of nowhere. He will need all of his strength, smarts, and courage to survive. Will he make it?

Target Words These words will help you understand how Robinson managed to survive his long adventure.

- **companion:** a friend or someone who keeps you company
  After being alone for a long time, Robinson wished for a companion.

- **stranded:** left alone in an unknown place with no way to escape
  Robinson is stranded on an island.

- **wits:** brains, cleverness
  Robinson must use his wits in order to survive.

Reader Tips Here's how to get the most out of this book.

- **Meet the Characters** Check out the characters on pages 6–7. Connect their names with their pictures as you read.

- **Problem/Solution** Think about each problem that Robinson faces. How does he try to solve it? Note whether or not he succeeds.

Meet the Characters

This story was written about 300 years ago. Back then, many parts of the world still had not been explored. This story takes place on a deserted island. The island is someplace between Europe and South America.

Robinson Crusoe

A young man who has always dreamed of going to sea. But his dream turns into a nightmare. He ends up alone on an island. Will he ever make it back home?

Friday

A prisoner of an enemy tribe.
He is almost their dinner.
Luckily, he makes a new
friend—just in time!

The Captain

The captain of a ship.
His crew is out for blood.
They've already taken over
his ship. Now they're ready
to dump him on an island.
Which island? Take a guess.

1

Off to Sea

**Robinson has always
dreamed of being a sailor.**

I was just 18 when I decided to go to sea. My parents were completely against it.

"We'll never see you again. Sailors leave home and they never come back," my father said bitterly.

My mother just looked at me and cried. She knew me well. She knew that I was going. It didn't matter what anyone said.

Ever since I was a boy, I'd wanted to sail the seas. I'd seen sailors come back with pockets full of gold. They threw their money around town like kings. I'd also heard their tales of adventure. They told of pirates, wild storms, and giant whales. That was the life for me. I was going, no matter what anyone said.

It was raining the night I snuck out of my house. I took nothing but a small bag slung over my shoulder. I headed down the empty streets to the docks. My ship was leaving in an hour.

I'd spoken to the captain the week before. He'd agreed to take me on. We were headed for Brazil, thousands of miles from the little English town where I grew up. I was ready— readier than I'd ever been for anything.

When I reached the dock, the first mate greeted me and shook my hand.

"Welcome to our ship, Robinson Crusoe," he said.

I stepped onto the boat. At last, I was a sailor!

I didn't know then what adventures life on the sea would bring. I also didn't know my father's words would turn out to be true. I would never see my parents again.

Heads Up!

Robinson wants to go to sea. How do his parents feel about this? Compare their feelings to Robinson's.

2

A Deadly Storm

Robinson's ship is rocked by a hurricane.
Will he make it out alive?

That first night on board the ship, the rain came down hard. The winds were strong. The ship tossed back and forth on the waves. The sails flapped in the wind. I wished I was home.

My stomach turned inside out. I leaned over the rail more than once. Finally, after hours of **misery,** I fell asleep below deck.

When morning came, the sky was clear and blue. I breathed a sigh of relief.

"Good morning, Crusoe," the first mate said, holding back a smile. "I must say, though, you look a little green."

"Quite a storm last night," I replied.

The first mate was silent. Then he let out a huge, roaring laugh.

"My boy, that was nothing. It was only a sprinkle, a tiny shower," he said. "One day, you'll see a real storm. But that wasn't it."

Over the next few weeks, our ship traveled many miles over the sea. As we sailed, I learned more and more. The crew taught me to raise the sails and pump water from the hold.

Soon, I noticed that my shipmates had stopped joking. Their voices were edgy with fear. For days, the weather had been threatening a storm. It was **hurricane** season.

Then one night, it happened. The sky filled with black clouds. The wind tore at the sails as we struggled to bring them down. Waves taller than buildings threw us back and forth. One **monstrous** wave towered over us and then smashed down onto the deck.

As the ship flooded with water, I grabbed onto a post. I hung onto it for dear life.

Heads Up!

Robinson and his shipmates have a big problem. What is it?

Robinson holds on as two sailors are blown overboard.

Before my eyes, two sailors were swept from the deck into the churning sea. I thought I would be next.

"Robinson, Robinson," I heard the captain yelling. "Get below!"

I scrambled for the door and ran down the stairs. We huddled in the captain's cabin through the night, not knowing if the ship would be able to outlast the storm. Why hadn't I listened to my father!

In the morning, the winds calmed a little. We opened the cabin door and climbed back up the stairs. The first man on deck saw something in the distance.

"Land ho!" he yelled in his loudest voice.

But before the rest of us could take a look, we felt a terrific jolt. The ship stopped. It rocked sideways and then fell backwards. All of us were thrown back down the stairs into the cabin.

The ship had struck something—rocks, perhaps, or a sandbar. We were stuck. When the winds picked up, the waves could easily smash our ship to pieces. Quickly, the captain made up his mind.

"To the lifeboat," he said. "This ship is going down. We've got to try and make it to land. It's our only chance."

Frantically, we lifted the lifeboat over the side of the ship and scrambled into it.

Pulling the oars, we tried to steer our tiny boat. When a wave lifted us up, we could see the shore. It was a distant line straight ahead. Then we fell deep down into a watery valley. The land disappeared as we looked straight into a wall of dark, gray water.

It may sound strange, but I wasn't really scared. There was no time to think. I could only pull, pull, pull at my oar.

Suddenly, a gigantic wave hit our lifeboat. We were all thrown overboard. My mouth filled with salt water as I started sinking to the bottom of the ocean.

Heads Up!

Look up the word **frantically** *in the glossary. What does that tell you about how the men are acting?*

But I'm a strong swimmer. I aimed straight for the water's surface. I kept swimming toward the light until I thought my lungs would burst. Finally, my head poked above the waves. I was no longer thinking about whether I would live or die. I just swam.

The waves lifted me, tossed me, and buried me. But I swam as fast and hard as I could. I swam until I felt a sandy floor beneath me.

When the water was shallow enough, I stood up and ran. I ran through the pounding surf to the beach. I didn't stop. I didn't pause. I ran until I knew no wave could catch me and drag me back into the ocean's deadly grip. I ran until the sand under my feet gave way to grass and rocks. Then I collapsed.

3

All Alone!

Will Robinson make it on his own?

When I finally raised my head and looked out at the pounding surf, I could barely make out my ship. It seemed so far away! How had I made it to shore?

I longed to find my shipmates. But after searching the beach and the waves, I realized the awful truth. I was the only one left alive.

Where was I? What should I do? I was completely alone. I had no food, no water, and my clothes were ripped to shreds. I tried to stay calm and figure out what to do first. My throat was horribly parched from sea salt. The first thing I needed was water.

Scrambling through the bushes, I saw a small stream. I buried my face in the cool, fresh water, gulping it down.

"What should I do next?" I wondered. I needed to find shelter—a place to spend the night. A few yards away, I found a large tree. It was thick with vines and matted leaves. Climbing into its branches, I found a place where I could curl up. Here, I thought, I might be safe from any man or beast. In seconds, I was asleep.

When the warm sun woke me up, I climbed down from my tree and headed back to the beach. The sea was now as smooth as glass.

The tide was low, making it easy for me to walk almost all the way to the ship. Tears rolled from my eyes as I grew near. It hadn't broken apart after all! If we had only stayed aboard, my shipmates would have survived! But there was nothing I could do about it now.

—Heads Up!—

Robinson finds water and a place to sleep for the night. What problems do you think he will have to solve next?

I knew I would have to use my **wits** to survive. I needed supplies. What was left on the ship could help keep me alive. I swam out and climbed aboard. The ship's kitchen was my first stop. Somehow it had stayed dry. I found some old biscuits and stuffed them in my mouth.

I needed a way to get the supplies to land. I found a saw and cut down the wooden **mast** and chopped it into pieces. Then I used rope to tie the pieces together. I dropped my raft over the side and saw that it floated well. It wouldn't carry much. But if I made enough trips, I could get everything I wanted to shore.

First, I loaded all the food—bread, cheese, rice, sugar, tea, and dried meat. Then I grabbed the swords and guns.

After that, I rounded up the ship's dogs and cats. They would be my only **companions** for a very long time. When I finally reached the shore, it was late in the afternoon.

My next mission was to find out more about this place. Where was I? Was I on an island? Had I made it all the way to South America, where our ship had been headed?

Robinson Crusoe rescues animals from the ship to keep him company on the island.

Climbing a nearby hill, I found the answer. I was on an island. As far as I could see, there were no towns, buildings, tents, or fires. There were no signs of people anywhere. I was alone in the middle of the sea on a **deserted** island.

Since there was no place I could go for help, I got to work. I made a tent using a piece of the ship's sail. And to protect myself and my food, I built a wall out of boxes and surrounded the tent. It would do for now. Then I crawled inside with my dogs and cats and went to sleep.

Heads Up!

Robinson has learned that he is alone on the island. What do you think he'll do next? What would you do?

My Island Home

Robinson builds a home to call his own.

I made twelve trips out to the ship in all. It took me almost two weeks, but I grabbed tools, nails, rope, scissors, cloth, and paper. I even came across a **telescope.**

On one trip to the ship, I found the captain's gold. I chuckled as I loaded the bag of gold onto my raft. In England, people would kill for it. Here, it was useless. But I took it anyway.

I had food, and I had water. Now I needed a sturdy home. I might be here for a while, until rescuers came, if they came. I explored the island until I found the best place.

It was a flat piece of ground on the side of a hill. There was water nearby, it was shaded from the sun, and it had a clear view of the ocean. I could keep watch for passing ships.

Steep cliffs were behind me. That made it impossible for creatures to sneak up and attack. And there was a small cave in the hill, which I could use as part of my home.

I set to work. I drew a large half circle in the ground around my cave. This would mark my yard. Then, I used my axe to chop down trees and my saw to cut off branches. Soon, I had a large pile of wooden poles. I drove them into the line I had marked in the ground.

With a wall surrounding my little yard, I felt safer. Neither man nor animal could get over the wall. But I could, using a ladder I had made.

Inside the walls of my yard, I built a large tent. I used pieces of sail. I used two layers to keep out the rain. Even in the strongest storm, I would stay dry. I hung a hammock I had taken from the ship. That's what I used for my bed.

Heads Up!

Robinson builds a wall around his yard for protection. Why does he build a ladder?

I used the cave as my kitchen. It was cool and dry. Here I could store my food.

When I had finished my work, I felt proud. This wasn't merely a house, it was a well-furnished **fortress.**

Each morning, I hunted for fresh food. There were birds and goats on this island, and vegetables and fruit as well. Although I had plenty of food from the ship, I wanted to use it slowly. I didn't know how long I'd be **stranded.**

To keep track of time, I made my own calendar. Each day, I cut a new notch into a wooden pole. Every seventh day, I made a larger notch to mark a week.

Building my fortress took many weeks. And making the furniture took even longer. I built a fireplace. I made a table on which to read and write. I built shelves in the walls of my caves.

At night, I would lie in my hammock with my dogs curled up beneath me. This was now my home sweet home.

Fever

A serious illness threatens Robinson's life.

At least it was home sweet home for a while. Soon, I grew tired of the same thing day after day. The weeks grew into months. The notches on my calendar were beginning to add up.

Then one morning in the ninth month, I awoke to a rainy day. It felt cold. That's when I knew there was something wrong. It was never cold on the island.

By the next day, I was shivering. The day after that, I had violent head pains. As the days went on, I got sicker and sicker. I lay in bed for more than a week. I was sick with a fever.

I did not eat. I grew weak. The fever continued. I couldn't even get out of bed to get water. I would die alone on this island. I knew this for sure.

One night, I had strange dreams brought on by the fever. I heard voices. They were so real that I spoke back to them. I woke sweating two or three times. I thought I saw someone. Was it real or only the dream? The long night of dreaming seemed to last for days. Maybe it did.

When I finally woke, I felt weak. But I was no longer feverish. I dragged myself to a stream where I drank and drank. Then I rested until I had gathered some more strength. I found some grapes by the stream and ate. Little by little, my health improved.

It took many weeks to fully recover, and I began to walk around the island slowly. My strength had not fully returned. So I kept my gun with me for protection.

I had survived the fever. And now, according to my calendar, I had been on the island for one year. Would I be stranded here forever?

Heads Up!

If you were alone for a year, how would that make you feel?

6

Cannibals!

Robinson is no longer alone on the island.
But are these the companions he wants?

After giving it a lot of thought, I realized there was only one thing left to do. I decided to build my own ship. I found the tallest cedar tree on the island and chopped it down. I worked day and night to make it into a canoe. I spent weeks carving it out and smoothing it down. When I was done, I had a fine, strong boat. But it was a boat made by a fool.

This boat weighed hundreds of pounds. No one man could carry or drag it, even with ropes or chains. And I had made my boat in the woods, at least two miles from shore. My fine boat would never make it to the water. It was completely useless. And all of my effort had been a waste of time.

I was disappointed. But soon I began to make other things.

I wanted baskets to carry fruit—limes, bananas, oranges, grapes—from a distant part of the island. But how do you make a basket? I reached back in my mind for a faraway memory—basket weavers working in the market in my town. Then, by trial and error, I made my own basket. I used soft green wooden twigs and wove them together.

I wanted candles so I could have some light in the evenings. I wanted pots to boil soup. I wanted an oven for baking bread. I wanted a kettle for making tea. It took a long time to figure out how to make each new thing. But it didn't matter. I had all the time in the world and nothing else to do.

Even as I settled into my new life, I didn't give up hope of rescue. Each day, I spent an hour high up in the cliffs. I searched the sea for passing ships, but I never saw one. This lonely island must have been far away from where ships traveled.

Two, and then five, years passed. I took up farming. Using seeds from the ship, I grew wheat, corn, and barley. No longer did I just hunt for animals. I bred them and kept them for milk.

Ten, twenty more years passed. I lacked almost nothing, except for one thing: human companionship. I was tired of being alone.

I had the grown pups and kittens of the animals I had saved. And I had a parrot named Polly. I had caught her and trained her to speak.

"Good morning, Robinson." "Are you well, Robinson?" "Food please, Robby."

It was a voice, but not a conversation.

Then one morning, as I was about to go fishing, I saw something strange on the beach. It was a footprint—a human footprint. And it wasn't mine.

─Heads Up!─
Robinson has just seen a footprint that isn't his. What does that mean? Who do you think it might be?

I stared at it, startled, shocked, and suddenly afraid. I ran home so quickly that my dogs could hardly keep up. I flew over the wall and hid, trembling in my cave.

For three days, I didn't come out. My mind was spinning. Who was this man? Was he still on the island? Was he alone? Was he a friend or enemy? Was he shipwrecked like me or was he a pirate? Would he try to kill me? Should I try to kill him first?

When I finally climbed the ladder back over my wall, my life was forever changed. No longer was my island a place apart from the world.

Over the next few days, I saw no further signs. I went about my life, but I was changed. The noise of a branch cracking made me jump. I imagined voices in the wind. I was always looking over my shoulder.

A few weeks after, I returned to the beach. Again, I was shocked, but now with pure horror. On the beach were the remains of a bonfire. The sand around it was scattered with footprints… and bones. But they weren't animal bones. They belonged to human beings!

Robinson finds bones on the beach.

My visitors had returned. And now I knew what they were. They were cannibals—humans who ate humans! They were using my island as a place to kill and eat.

Again, I ran back home. I cleaned my guns. I hid weapons in different places around the island. Never in my life had I thought of hurting another man. But if the cannibals came for me, I would be ready.

A month later, I spotted them from a distance. They were heading for the beach in long canoes. I could see five boats and about twenty men in all. There were too many to fight. So I decided to find a place where I could hide and watch them.

I crouched behind some rocks across the stream behind the beach. From there, I could safely watch and decide what to do.

When the boats reached the shore, the men began to build a bonfire on the beach. They were tall and armed with knives and clubs. One poor man was being held as a prisoner.

I had seen what was left of victims who had come before him. My heart filled with pity.

7

Friday

Robinson makes an unlikely friend.

The cannibals were busy getting ready for their ceremony. They weren't paying much attention to their prisoner. He must have used the time to loosen his ropes because, suddenly, he jumped up and broke free. With nothing to lose, the prisoner ran for his life. I watched as he came heading straight for the stream— toward me!

Three of the cannibals ran after him. The prisoner dove into the stream and climbed out on the other side. He was now only inches from where I was hiding. I knew I had to help him. There would be no more cannibalism here— not on my island!

Two of the cannibals had followed their victim into the stream. When they came out,

I jumped out from my hiding place behind the rock. I swung my rifle and hit one of them hard, knocking him to his knees.

I don't know who was more startled—the cannibals or the man they were trying to catch. All three looked at me in shock, as if I had dropped out of the sky.

Then I fired my gun straight into the air— once, twice, three times. Stunned by the noise, the two cannibals froze. Then they turned and jumped back into the stream.

I watched as they ran back to the beach. From a distance, I could see them talking wildly. Then the entire group hopped back into their boats and rowed away.

Their former prisoner was still standing next to me. He was wet and shaking.

I called him Friday.

Friday was the day that I had saved his life. I could think of no better name.

He kneeled down, trembling, not knowing who I was or what I planned to do. I spoke to him softly and smiled. Although he didn't know my language, he could see that I meant no harm.

Robinson saves Friday from the cannibals.

Slowly, he came closer, still on his knees. He moved his arms up and down. I could tell that he was thanking me for rescuing him.

I led him back up to my home and gave him something to eat—milk and bread and cheese. When was the last time that I had shared a meal with another person? It had been over twenty years! Friday ate greedily.

When he finished eating, he fell fast asleep.

Heads Up!

How does Robinson save Friday? What does he do first? Next?

8

Fast Friends

At last, Robinson finds a friend.

Friday was tall and not too large. I would guess he was about twenty-six years old. His hair was long and black, and his teeth were as white as ivory.

He soon proved to be the best company any man could want. He was gentle, kind, and good. To hear his voice was the finest music in the entire world.

At first, I couldn't understand a word he said. I simply enjoyed listening to the sound. To communicate, we would gesture, point, and draw pictures in the ground.

I showed him my daily routine: fetching water, milking goats, tending crops, gathering fruit, and making bread. When I took him hunting, I found out why the cannibals had fled so fast. Neither they nor their prisoner had ever seen a gun. Friday gasped when I shot a wild bird. He thought it was magic. To him it looked as if I waved a long stick, made a loud noise, and somehow a bird fell from the sky.

Soon Friday began to pick up my language, and I began to pick up his. As the months went by, we began to truly talk. We told each other about our faraway homes. We told each other about our families.

I was surprised to learn that Friday had been a cannibal, too, until he had come to live with me. He explained that cannibals only eat their enemies. He had been captured by another tribe.

After a while, Friday and I made plans to build a boat. But there seemed to be no hurry. Now that I had a companion on the island, I was more content. These were the best years I had had since I came to this lonely place.

Heads Up!

Why are the years with Friday Robinson's "best years" on the island?

9

The Mutineers

**Robinson finds a way off the island.
But he'll have to fight a few battles first.**

Friday's shouting awakened me.

"Robinson, Robinson," he yelled, waving the telescope in his hand. "Man they come. They come."

"The cannibals?" I asked. I was afraid they would return sooner or later.

"No," he said. "Your people. Man like you."

I grabbed the telescope and looked down at the sea. It was true. Far out on the waves was an English ship at anchor. Closer was a longboat being rowed toward my island. Eleven men were in the boat. I was confused. What was going on?

When the longboat landed on the beach, eight men got out. Then they lifted out three prisoners who had been tied up. The men wandered off to explore the island. The prisoners were left on the sand.

After the men had been gone for a while, Friday and I carefully snuck down from our fortress and approached the three prisoners.

"What is happening here?" I said.

The prisoners were surprised to see us. They looked at me with complete confusion.

"Are you a man, an angel, or a beast?" asked one of the prisoners.

"I am an Englishman," I said. "And I might be your friend. But first tell me your story and then we shall see. Quickly."

"I am the captain of that boat," he said. "These two are my first mate and a passenger. The rest of the crew has turned against me. They have taken over the ship. When they return they are going to kill us."

---**Heads Up!**---

Why do you think the captain asks Robinson if he is a man, angel, or beast?

"Maybe not," I replied. "But if I help you, you must help me in return."

"Anything," the captain swore. "I will be at your service forever."

"First," I told him, "you must obey my every command on this island. Second, when we get back to your ship, you must take Friday and myself back to England."

Instantly, the captain agreed. We untied the men, and Friday handed each of them a weapon.

Within moments, two of the **mutineers** strolled out of the forest. They appeared to be the leaders. The captain and the first mate fired their guns.

The leaders fell to the ground, hurt. The other mutineers ran out of the woods. They saw that their leaders were wounded. Then they saw the five of us with weapons. They surrendered without a fight.

Quickly, we tied their hands and led them away from the beach.

We placed the mutineers in my cave and bandaged the wounded. Then we sat down to dinner. I felt proud as the captain admired my home. I was also very excited. I was finally going back to England.

But we had one more problem to solve.

"The trouble," said the captain, "is that there are fifteen mutineers still on board the ship. Mutiny is a crime. They can be hanged for it, and they know it."

"So they won't give up easily," the first mate explained. "They'll be fighting for their lives."

I thought long and hard. Then I came up with a plan.

Heads Up!

What do you think Robinson will do next?

10

Victory

Will Robinson finally make it home?

Soon, another longboat left the ship and headed for the island. I had expected that. They were looking for the men who hadn't returned from the island. The captain studied the boat from the island with the telescope.

"I see ten men with rifles," he said. "Seven of them are bad. Three are good, but they are scared of the others."

"Fine," I said. "I know what to do."

When the longboat landed, Friday and the first mate began shouting from a spot in the forest. Eight men went off to investigate the noise. They left two to watch the boat. Staying on the move—and just out of sight—Friday and the first mate led the eight deeper and deeper into the woods.

Meanwhile, the captain and I stepped onto the beach with our guns pointed at the two who were left. Helpless, they immediately surrendered. One was a good man. He swore **loyalty** to the captain and joined our side. We gave him a gun. We tied up the other one and brought him to the cave.

Hours later, the eight finally found their way back to the beach. Friday and the first mate had led them in circles. They were worn out and confused. Where were the two men they'd left with the boat?

The longboat was now stuck in the sand. The tide had gone out. They couldn't go anywhere until high tide returned. So the eight men went to sleep on the beach.

When darkness fell, I had Friday and the captain fire several shots into the air. The tired mutineers jumped up in fear. Then I had our good man call out to their leader, a man named Tom Smith.

"Tom Smith!" he yelled. "Lay down your guns or be killed. I'm with the captain now. We have fifty armed men."

This, of course, was a lie. But in the dark, they couldn't know that.

"If we give up, we'll be hanged," Smith replied fearfully.

Then the captain spoke, "If you lay down your arms, I will spare your lives. Act now or we fire at once."

When the mutineers walked out of the woods, they were surprised to see only six of us. But it was too late.

The two other good men ran to the captain and begged for forgiveness. We tied the others up and led them to my cave.

High tide returned, and the captain and his group of five loyal sailors returned to the ship. Together they would fight the mutineers who were still on the ship.

Not longer after the captain left the island, Friday and I heard seven shots. This was the captain's signal that he was back in control.

We slept solidly during our last night on the island, tired from the day's events.

In the morning, the captain came back. First, he went to see the prisoners in the cave.

The captain calls to the mutineers and tricks them into
giving up.

He offered them a choice: return to England and face trial or stay on the island. Most of them chose to stay.

Then the captain signaled to me that it was time to go. He had brought me some clothing—a long shirt and trousers. It had been so long since I had worn proper clothes. They felt strange and stiff to me when I put them on.

Believe it or not, I took almost nothing from the island. I grabbed a goatskin cap, my bag of gold, and my parrot.

Then Friday and I walked toward the longboat that would take us to the ship.

I felt happy, excited, and just a little sad.

I had spent twenty-eight years, two months, and nineteen days on the island. Now, I was finally headed home.

Heads Up!

How does Robinson feel about leaving the island? Would you feel the same way?

Meet the Author

Daniel Defoe

(1660–1731)

Daniel Defoe based *Robinson Crusoe* on the experiences of a real person, Alexander Selkirk. In 1704, Selkirk lived on a deserted island for more than four years before he was rescued. It was pretty amazing that he survived.

But what Defoe did was pretty amazing, too. He helped invent the kind of book we call a novel. *Robinson Crusoe* is one of the first books written that tells a realistic story using plain language.

At first, Defoe had trouble finding a publisher. But the book was finally published in 1719. And it has been popular ever since. It even spawned two sequels.

Defoe earned about $15 for his book. (That was a lot more money 300 years ago!) But the publisher still got a pretty good deal. *Robinson Crusoe* turned out to be one of the most famous stories of all time.

Glossary

companion *(noun)* a friend or someone who keeps you company (p. 18)

deserted *(adjective)* a place where no humans live (p. 20)

fortress *(noun)* a place built to withstand attack, often built by the military (p. 23)

frantically *(adverb)* desperately, quickly (p. 14)

hurricane *(noun)* a violent storm (p. 11)

loyalty *(noun)* the state of being devoted and true (p. 43)

mast *(noun)* a pole that supports a sail (p. 18)

misery *(noun)* unhappiness and sorrow (p. 10)

monstrous *(adjective)* huge and horrible (p. 11)

mutineer *(noun)* a person who revolts against someone in charge (p. 40)

stranded *(adjective)* left alone in an unknown place with no way to escape (p. 23)

telescope *(noun)* a tool that makes things that are far away seem larger and closer (p. 21)

wits *(noun)* brains, cleverness (p. 18)